Chester the Cat's High-Flying Dream

Jo A Forrest

© 2024 Jo A Forrest. All rights reserved.

No part of this book may be reproduced, stored in a retrieval system, or transmitted by any means without the written permission of the author.

AuthorHouse™
1663 Liberty Drive
Bloomington, IN 47403
www.authorhouse.com
Phone: 833-262-8899

Because of the dynamic nature of the Internet, any web addresses or links contained in this book may have changed since publication and may no longer be valid. The views expressed in this work are solely those of the author and do not necessarily reflect the views of the publisher, and the publisher hereby disclaims any responsibility for them.

Any people depicted in stock imagery provided by Getty Images are models, and such images are being used for illustrative purposes only.
Certain stock imagery © Getty Images.

This book is printed on acid-free paper.

ISBN: 979-8-8230-3337-4 (sc)
ISBN: 979-8-8230-3335-0 (hc)
ISBN: 979-8-8230-3336-7 (e)

Library of Congress Control Number: 2024923666

Print information available on the last page.

Published by AuthorHouse 11/18/2024

authorHOUSE®

This book is dedicated to my son Eric, his son Mason and wife Yasmin. Eric worked hard to fulfill his dream of becoming a pilot. It was dedication, hard work and the continued support of his family that made it possible. We are so proud!

In the small town of Chickahominy Falls, lived a funny, energetic, and curious cat named Chester. He had big blue eyes, orange and white fur and always wore a compass on his collar.

Unlike other cats who loved napping in the sun or chasing birds, Chester daydreamed about soaring high above the clouds.

When Chester was a kitten, his mom and dad always read him books about adventure, kindness and making dreams come true. He knew one day he would make his parents proud.

Most days Chester would sit on the highest branch of the tallest tree, gazing at the sky and imagining himself in a shiny big airplane, navigating through the fluffy white clouds.

He loved to listen to the stories of old Pilot Pete, a retired pilot who lived next door.

Pilot Pete has flown all over the world and had a treasure trove of tales about his adventures.

One sunny afternoon, as Chester sat listening to Pilot Pete, he gathered the courage to share his dream. "Pilot Pete, I want to become a pilot just like you!" he declared, his eyes sparkling with determination.

Pilot Pete chuckled kindly. "Well, Chester, it takes a lot of hard work, courage, and knowledge to become a pilot. Are you ready for the challenge?"

"Yes, I am!" Chester replied eagerly.

News of Chester's ambition spread quickly through Chickahominy Falls. The other animals were skeptical. "A cat, a pilot? Impossible!" they scoffed. "Cats are meant for napping and purring, not flying planes!"

Despite their doubts, Chester was determined. The first step, Pilot Pete told Chester, is "we need to do a Discovery Flight. During a Discovery Flight, you will get hands-on experience, learn about pre-flight checks, take-off, landing and other fun, but important things a pilot must do." Chester immediately started purring and chasing his tail with excitement, "Yes, yes, let's go".

As Pilot Pete expected, Chester loved it. He loved everything about it. He loved the beautiful blue sky and flying through the fluffy white clouds that he had gazed up at for so long. He felt free like he imagined birds must feel. It was thrilling and fun. He knew after that day he wouldn't want to be anything other than a pilot.

Pilot Pete took him under his wing, teaching him everything he needed to know about flying. Chester studied hard, learning about engines, weather patterns, and navigation.

Chester loved everything he was learning. The part he was the most excited about was the simulator. He knew Pilot Pete loved to use the simulator; he always says it's like flying in a real plane.

Pilot Pete's simulator was set up in his garage and he told Chester "You come practice anytime you'd like".

Chester climbed onto the simulator seat, and with a paw on the joystick, he started his first virtual flight. He quickly learned to navigate the skies.

He dodged birds, balloons, and even other airplanes. It was hard at first, but he was loving it, but he knew he must practice every day to be a great pilot like Pilot Pete.

Days turned into weeks, and weeks into months. Chester's paws ached from endless practice, but he never gave up. He knew that to achieve his dream, he had to stay committed and work hard.

Finally, the day came when Chester was ready for his first real flight. The whole town gathered at the small airstrip to watch. They whispered among themselves, still unsure if Chester could really do it.

Chester took a deep breath, climbed into the cockpit, completed his checklist, and started the engine. The plane roared to life, Chester taxied to the runway, very excited and a little nervous for his first solo flight.

As the plane gained speed, Chester's heart pounded with excitement. He pulled back on the controls, and the plane lifted off the ground, soaring into the sky.

His neighbors and friends watched in awe as Chester expertly guided the plane through the air, performing loops and twirls with grace and precision. "He's really doing it!" they exclaimed, their doubt turning into awe.

Up in the sky, Chester felt a sense of freedom and triumph like never before. He had done it! He had proven to everyone, including himself, that dreams could come true with hard work and determination.

After landing smoothly back on the airstrip, Chester was greeted with cheers and applause. Even the skeptics couldn't help but admire his courage and determination.

From that day on, Chester became the town's beloved pilot, taking passengers on exciting aerial tours and inspiring others to pursue their dreams, no matter how impossible they might seem. He proved that with determination, hard work, and a little bit of faith, anything was possible.

Now in Chickahominy Falls, the sky was no longer the limit, thanks to a brave cat named Chester who dared to dream big and take to the sky.

Printed in the USA
CPSIA information can be obtained
at www.ICGtesting.com
CBHW041804291124
18172CB00045B/1183